GW00864369

For Sam

British Library Cataloguing in Publication Data

Anderson, Scoular
    The enormous chocolate pudding.
    I. Title
    823′.914 [J]

    ISBN 0-340-49107-8

Text and illustrations copyright © Scoular Anderson 1987

First published 1987 by J. M. Dent & Sons Ltd
This edition first published 1989 by Picture Knight

Published by Hodder and Stoughton Paperbacks,
a division of Hodder and Stoughton Ltd,
Mill Road, Dunton Green, Sevenoaks, Kent TN13 2YE
Editorial office: 47 Bedford Square, London WC1B 3DP

Printed in Denmark

All rights reserved

Scoular Anderson

The Enormous Chocolate Pudding

Picture Knight

From the moment he climbed out of bed, the King of Sirocco knew it would be one of those days when everything went wrong. "I feel terrible," he groaned. "I can tell it's going to be a difficult day!"

The King stumbled down to breakfast to find indeed that nothing was right. His egg was cold, the toast was burnt, and when he took a sip of tea, he discovered there was salt in it. "What's wrong with you all today?" he shouted to his courtiers and servants. Not one was willing to reply.

"Well?" roared the King impatiently. At last the butler spoke up. "It's the enormous chocolate pudding in the garden, Sire. It seems to have upset everyone."

"Enormous chocolate pudding in the garden? Don't talk such rubbish!" exclaimed the King.

But when the King went out on to his balcony he found the view across the garden completely blocked by what looked remarkably like chocolate pudding.

Rushing downstairs, he cried, "There's an enormous chocolate pudding blocking my view. There's an enormous pudding where a pudding shouldn't be. Get rid of it!"

The King summoned the best cooks in the land. "You know all about puddings," he said. "There's an enormous pudding in the garden. Get rid of it or I'll have your heads in stew."

Trembling, the cooks set to work.

Out came their bowls and out came their spoons. Out came their ladles and out came their scales. The cooks looked through all their cookery books but they could find no recipe for removing an enormous chocolate pudding.

"Well?" said the King. Only one cook dared to speak.

"With all respects, and begging Your Majesty's pardon," she stuttered, "we can *cook* things but we can't *uncook* things once they're made. Perhaps the pudding belongs to a giant. Have you thought of asking a giant to remove it?"

Immediately the King summoned some neighbouring giants.
"A pudding as large as this must belong to you," said the King. "Get rid of it or I'll have your heads for footstools!"

Scratching their heads, the giants set to work.

They rolled up their sleeves and they flexed their muscles. They did press-ups and warming-up jumps. They pushed and they pulled, and they shouted HEAVE HO! but they couldn't budge the pudding.

"Well?" said the King.

"We're very good at tug-o'-wars and lifting weights," complained one of the giants, "but puddings are almost impossible to shift. They are slippery and they wobble, and it's very difficult to get to grips with them. I think this is a job for the guards."

So the King summoned the guards.
"Get rid of that pudding," said the King, "or I'll have your heads for cannon balls."
"At once, Sire," said the captain of the guards.
"We'll have it taken away before you can say *hot chocolate sauce*."

So the captain shouted orders and the trumpets blew. Soldiers laid rails and brought engines. They harnessed horses and fixed chains, but still the enormous chocolate pudding failed to be moved even an inch.

"Well?" said the King, by now purple in the face with fury. The captain clicked his heels and saluted. "I'm afraid this is not within our duties, Sire. We cannot move enormous chocolate puddings."

The King was enraged. "I refuse to have an enormous chocolate pudding sitting in my garden a moment longer!" Then he added in a small voice, "Can no one help?" because he was really a very gentle man at heart.

Suddenly the court jester had a good idea. He whispered it to the maid, who whispered it to the gardener, who whispered it to the housekeeper, who whispered it to the captain of the guards, who whispered it to the Queen, who whispered it to the butler, who whispered it to the King, who smiled for the first time that day and said, "What a brilliant suggestion! Why didn't we think of that before?"

When there was no longer a spoonful of pudding left and the King had licked the last bit of chocolate from his moustache, he said, "Wasn't it a good idea to eat the pudding? But, of course, nobody is better than I am at thinking up good ideas!"

The jester winked at the palace courtiers and servants and said, "I think it would be a good idea if we all crossed our fingers and wished. That way we might get another pudding."
"Don't talk such rubbish," said the King and, taking the Queen by the arm, he led her back to the palace.
But those watching closely could see that the King had his fingers very tightly crossed.